PRINCESS LEIA ORGASMA: SEXY CONCUBINE

RILEY ROSE

BOOK TWO IN THE PRINCESS LEIA ORGASMA SERIES

Copyright © 2025 Riley Rose

Cover Design by Mahinoor eBooks

All rights reserved. No part of this publication may be reproduced, distributed, or transmitted in any form or by any means without the the prior written permission of the author, except in the case of brief quotations for review purposes.

This is a work of fiction and any resemblance to real people, places, or situations is coincidental.

Books in Series

Book 1 - Princess Leia Orgasma: A Sexy Sci-Fi Parody

Sign-Up for my E-Mail List to Stay Up-To-Date on New Releases!

Visit RileyRoseErotica.com for more sexy stories!

Chapter 1

"I want his dick," Lay Me whispered.

"No me!" Boobla replied.

Leia batted their hands away. "Hey, he's my lover. I get to ride his nerf herder cock."

They were standing before Han, still frozen in carbonite in Jabba's palace, getting ready to implement round two in Leia's efforts to sexually thaw her favorite scoundrel. But this time she had brought her two Twe'erk friends. And they were both eager to get at Han.

"Okay," the blue-skinned Lay Me replied. "We'll grind against him while you suck him off."

The green-tinted Boobla nodded. "Good idea."

It was dark in the palace, the moonlight coming through the skylights the only thing illuminating the three gorgeous women. Even though Leia had tried this plan before, she was hopeful multiple nude female bodies would defrost Han more quickly.

Jabba had caught her when she initially tried to thaw Han by fucking him. But she had earned the crime lord's trust over the past week. But only by engaging in a lot of embarrassing activities.

She had to dance for Jabba in her skimpy slave-girl outfit after Boobla and Lay Me taught her their hip-shaking Twe'erk moves. She figured she could put those moves to good use when she got Han alone in the bedroom. Or when negotiating with planets she hoped would join the Rebellion.

She also had to fuck Jabba. A lot. He constantly slobbered his huge tongue across her pussy and ass. And was constantly making Leia cum. Which is why she was so conflicted: she hated degrading herself by being his concubine, but she loved the powerful orgasms he gave her. Who knew a gross slug would be so good at pleasuring women?

The most embarrassing thing, however, was that Jabba loved stripping and spanking Leia in front of his entourage. He used his tongue to undo the clasp of her golden brassiere and to yank down her breechcloth. He was very skilled with that tongue of his, so skilled that he could spank Leia much harder than most species could with their hands.

Leia's face and butt turned very red during these spanking sessions. It was mortifying to have her clothes ripped off and be disciplined in front of such a motley crew. Well, it would have been mortifying in front of anyone. But Jabba said a princess needed to be reminded of her place. And that place was as his sex slave.

The palace denizens never seemed to get tired of gazing upon Leia's nude body. So while she was often embarrassed, she was also flattered. And more than a little turned on. She'd be lying if she said she didn't get wet every time Jabba spanked her. She was learning she had a thing for kinky discipline. She wondered if Han would be into giving her some spankings for being a naughty princess. She sure hoped so. She needed him to bend her over the holochess table on his ship and slap her bare booty. What?! She did? Leia surprised herself with her dirty thoughts. Apparently, all the hours she spent fucking Jabba, Boobla, and Lay Me had made her incredibly horny.

But the person she was most horny for was standing in front of her: Han, the love of her life. She would put up with any degrading treatment if it meant she could free him and spend the rest of her life in his arms.

And this time she had come up with a sneakier plan. Boobla and Lay Me had procured a sleeping powder, which Leia had snuck into Jabba's drink while she was tail fucking him. Whenever she rode his massive appendage, his bulbous eyes rolled into the back of his head, so he had no hope of seeing her sneaky trick. Of course, he had cum all over her, but Leia had gotten used to that. She spent much of her days sticky. Fortunately, the Twe'erk ladies would clean her each morning, and their cleaning techniques were lovely. And sexy! Leia had come to regard the two women as close friends. And she was just as determined to free them from Jabba's clutches as herself and Han.

Speaking of the Twe'erk hotties, Lay Me and Boobla were

getting restless. "On your knees princess," the blue girl said. "Scoundrels love being sucked off by beautiful sluts."

Boobla nodded vigorously. "And you've proven what a great slut you are."

"Um, thanks," Leia replied, blushing. That hadn't really been her goal, but she knew the sensual alien girls meant it as a compliment. And she was eager to put her mouth around Han's cock, even frozen in carbonite. "Okay, here goes."

She ran her tongue along Han's shaft. It was cool, but Leia knew she could warm it up.

She twirled her tongue around the tip of his penis, following the instructions the Twe'erk ladies had taught her. They were highly skilled in the arts of pleasing both men and women.

Leia thought she felt Han's penis twitch. It was probably just her imagination as he was fully frozen, but maybe her ministrations were working. She was sure the theory about unthawing someone from carbonite through sex would prove true. It had to, since she couldn't get the carbonite console to work and had no idea how to fix it.

She wrapped her lips around Han's head and put her fingers on his thighs.

"Put your hands in your lap," Lay Me instructed.

"Guys like it when girls look submissive," Boobla added.

Leia did as instructed, placing her hands against her bare legs, which were pressed together. She was more than happy to be submissive for Han. She might be confident and commanding among her fellow Rebels, but she secretly wanted to be dominated in the bedroom. At least by one particular scruffy scoundrel.

She moved her mouth back and forth on Han's frozen cock. It felt a little strange, not tasting his warm flesh, but she didn't mind. It made her feel connected to him, like she was his dirty princess whore. *Yes, Han, I'll be a naughty slut for you!* That thought inspired Leia to go harder.

And that inspired Lay Me and Boobla to get in on the action. They rubbed their naked bodies along either side of Han, bouncing their boobs against his chest and grinding their pussies against his thighs.

Leia glanced up at them. She knew Han would have been in heaven if he had been awake: three women pleasuring him at once was a dream come true.

The Twe'erk girls decided to help Leia in her oral commitment. They snatched her hair with their long leeku and yanked her head back and forth, forcing her to mouth fuck Han much harder.

Leia sputtered into his cock and made unintelligible noises. Her lover had a big dick, and it was tough work taking the whole thing. But it felt good kneeling before him, feeling like her sole duty was pleasuring his space sword.

She felt his penis get warmer. She motioned to Lay Me and Boobla to let her have some air.

The girls released their grip on Leia's long locks.

"I think it's working," she told them excitedly, though she made sure not to yell. While Jabba should be in a deep snooze thanks to the sleep agent Leia had slipped him, the other palace denizens could be roused more easily.

"Great," Lay Me replied. "That means it's time to give him your princess pussy."

Leia leapt up. She loved giving Han her princess pussy. At least she did the first time she fucked his carbonite cock. He had felt wonderful inside her, but she had been so loud she woke the whole palace. She would have to rein in her submissive screams this time.

She moved her slit up along the head of his penis, easily getting herself wet. Then she eased onto him, sliding all the way to the base of his shaft.

"Ohhhhh Han," she moaned into his chest. "You belong inside me." She pressed her lips against him to muffle her sounds. He was so big it was almost impossible not to cry out when he penetrated her.

"Wow, his cock looks great inside you," Boobla whispered.

"Your ass is trembling from how much he's filling you," Lay Me commented.

Leia blushed. It was true: her buttocks were shaking as her pussy tried to adjust to Han's big bantha meat.

She placed her hands against his chest and moved her hips back and forth. He slid in and out of her, the friction heating up Leia's tight pussy.

The Twe'erk girls helped out, grinding their curvy bodies against both Han and Leia.

Their head-tails roamed Leia's skin, focusing on her firm butt, each girl claiming one cheek for her own.

The butt massage prompted Leia to fuck Han even harder. She sped up, her pussy squishing every time she impaled herself on Han's cock.

Leia did her best to stifle her moans, but it was hard. If Han was this good when he was frozen, Leia couldn't imagine how wonderful it would feel when he fucked her while fully animated.

"It's working," Boobla said. "I feel the carbonite warming."

"Tell him how much you want him," Lay Me suggested. The two alien girls seemed to be as much into Leia fucking Han as Leia was herself. They really were great friends!

Leia gazed at Han's face. It was contorted into a pained expression from the carbonite freezing. That just made Leia more determined to free him and reward him by fucking his brains out every night. He deserved to be attended to after serving as Jabba's trophy for so long. "Han, I want you so bad," she whispered desperately. "I want you to take me every night and make me your princess slut. I'll do whatever dirty thing you want!" Leia was surprised by her confession. She was becoming so naughty. And she kind of liked it.

"That's it," Lay Me praised her. "You're really turning him

on."

"He's definitely heating up," Boobla agreed.

Leia did feel warmth from her lover's body. At first, she thought it was just her own heat, which was intense based on how hard she was fucking him, but Han's own warmth emanated through her nipples. That meant her plan was working. If she kept riding him vigorously, she would be able to free him. Wild sex was the solution to all problems! Okay, maybe she was getting ahead of herself. But it was definitely the solution to this problem.

Lay Me's head tendril poked at Leia's back door. "Princess, have you ever had a leeku up your butt?"

"W… what?" Leia asked in surprise.

"They fit nice and snug in girls' hineys," Boobla told her.

"I… um…" It was hard to focus with Han's cock dominating her. "I've never had anything up my butt."

Lay Me rubbed her tentacle along Leia's ass. "Our leeku will be perfect. The tips are nice and small and will be a good warm-up for when your space pirate shoves his space cock up there."

"What?!" Leia gasped, forgetting she was supposed to be quiet. "Y… you think Han will want to have anal sex with me?"

"Of course," Boobla replied. "Everyone expects princesses to take it up the butt."

Leia let out another gasp. How did she not know all these

common stereotypes about princesses? Should she have been practicing getting fucked up the ass the past few years? Being raised in a royal family was wonderful, but it also sheltered her from knowing important facts about life: like how she needed to learn how to take it up her rear end.

Lay Me ran her blue tendril between Leia's ass cheeks. "You'll have your man for life if you let him butt fuck you."

Leia's eyes lit up. "Really?" She wanted to mate with Han for life, wanted to fight by his side, make love to him after fierce battles, and playfully tease him while she lay cuddled in his arms.

And it wasn't like she had never thought about what it would feel like to take it in her rear entry port. But she thought proper princesses didn't do that. Who knew it was expected of all young royals? She had so much to learn.

"O... okay, you can explore my butt," she told the girls. "But be gentle, okay?"

Boobla caressed her back. "Don't worry. We'll take care of you."

"While you take care of that massive cock," Lay Me said.

Leia took care of the massive cock, her juices dripping from her burning hot pussy. Lay Me and Boobla took advantage of that by dipping their leeku in Leia's juices and getting them nice and lubricated for their anal probing.

The blue beauty was the first to sample Leia's rear, pressing the tip of her head-tail against the princess's opening.

"Relax your ass," she told Leia. "It'll feel better going in."

Leia unclenched her butt muscles, not realizing how nervous she was about her first anal. But Boobla and Lay Me massaged her body, making her feel safe and ready to try anything.

The blue leeku pressed firmly against Leia's ass until it penetrated her.

"Ohhhh!" Leia yelped in shock-surprise. She knew it was coming, but she still wasn't ready for exactly how it would feel. It was strange: not exactly painful, slightly uncomfortable, but also kind of cozy.

She wiggled her butt, trying to get used to the foreign visitor.

Lay Me patted Leia's hips. "Don't worry. It always feels weird at first."

"But it's fantastic once you get used to it," Boobla assured her.

Leia nodded. These two had obviously had a lot of experience in having their Twe'erk tushes explored. Leia wondered if there was anything about sex they didn't know. She had found perfect tutors to help her explore her kinky side.

Lay Me probed deeper, eliciting another gasp from the princess. Leia's ass contracted around the tendril, more eagerly welcoming it now that it had gotten more used to it.

"Doesn't that feel nice and warm in your butt?" Lay Me

whispered in Leia's ear.

"Uh... uh huh," Leia replied breathlessly. Her friend's leeku emanated a cozy warmth, letting Leia know it belonged in her rear end. Leia wasn't going to argue with that logic, so she begged Lay Me to fuck her ass while she continued riding Han.

The Twe'erk girl pumped Leia's booty, slowly at first, but then increasing speed as the princess got used to having her ass filled.

"I think she likes it," Boobla commented, staring at Leia's desperate sex faces.

"She loves it. Don't you, Princess?" Lay Me shoved her leeku in even farther.

"Fuck, I love it!" Leia confessed. She thought getting pussy fucked was amazing. She never realized getting fucked in both holes would be so much better. She wondered if getting all three orifices filled would be the ultimate experience.

Boobla must have read her mind: she placed one of her leeku to Leia's mouth, tickling her lips. "You're being a little too loud, Princess, Suck on this." She shoved her green tendril past Leia's lips.

"Mrmph!" Leia gasped as she took the luscious leeku. It was coated in Leia's juices, which made her feel quite naughty. She had gotten a lot of experience tasting herself thanks to her Twe'erk friends.

"All three holes filled," Lay Me commented. "That's how

all princess sluts like it."

Leia tried to reply but she was too busy sucking off Boobla. And smashing her pussy on Han's dick. And getting ass blasted by Lay Me. She was learning a lot about slutty princesses. And learning a lot about how to be the sluttiest of them all. Which wasn't her goal coming to Jabba's palace, but she told herself it wasn't a bad side mission. She couldn't deny how much she enjoyed the past week's sexual adventures. And definitely couldn't deny how much she loved the triple fucking she was getting. The only thing that could make it better was if…

As if once again reading her mind, Lay Me snatched Leia's wrists and pinned them behind her back. She knew the princess got even hornier when she was bound and helpless.

Leia surrendered to the feelings of ultimate bliss, her pussy burning, her ass throbbing, and her mouth straining to take all of Boobla.

The slab of carbonite radiated heat, and an orange glow surrounded Han.

"It's working!" Boobla exclaimed.

"I bet if you cum, you'll fully free him," Lay Me advised.

Leia wasn't sure if spraying her juices across Han's cock would help unthaw him, but she desperately needed to cum. Every cell of her body seemed to be screaming for orgasmic release. "Y… yes, I want to cum so bad!" That wasn't a very princessy thing to say, but Leia had done a lot of non-princessy things on this mission.

Boobla had removed her leeku to let Leia confess her sluttiness, but had another good use for it: rubbing Leia's clit.

That was the final piece needed to unleash Leia's climax. "I love scruffy nerf herders!!" she screamed, her body shaking as she succulently squirted all over Han.

He fully thawed and broke free of the carbonite.

He fell forward, landing on top of Leia, his cock fully impaling her.

And then he came inside her.

Leia gasped. She wrapped her arms around his neck and her legs around his hips, clutching him tightly. *Oh yes, Han! Fill me with your scoundrel space seed!* Leia had dreamed about this moment: Han's rugged body on top of her, spreading his most intimate gift inside her. It wasn't exactly how she had pictured it, being in a gangster's palace and having to free her lover from carbonite. But it was still wonderful.

Han thrust against her, emptying his space balls. He sure had a lot of sperm. But it made sense: he was frozen for months and probably had a ton of semen to unload.

Leia was happy to accept all of it. She brought her lips to his, kissing him deeply.

Han gasped after their lips parted, timed perfectly with his last sperm salvo. "Who... who are you?"

"Someone who loves you," Leia replied, kissing him again.

"Leia!" he exclaimed. A huge smile crossed his shivering

face. "I... I can't see."

"It's hibernation sickness," she explained. One side effect of coming out of carbonite was temporarily blindness. "Don't worry, it will fade."

He groped for her face, touching her cheeks like she was an oasis in the deserts of Titooine. "Did... I just cum inside you?"

"Um, yes." She blushed. "The only way I could free you is by, well, fucking you."

"When did you start talking like a space pirate?" he asked.

She bit her lip. "It's, uh, been an eventful week. And I've had some naughty influences."

On cue, Boobla and Lay Me knelt beside them.

"I'm Lay Me," the blue alien said. "You're mated to the most beautiful princess in the galaxy."

Han smiled. "I sure am." That got him another huge smooch from Leia.

"And one of the horniest," Boobla added. "She's been obsessed with your dick."

Han raised an eyebrow. "Really?"

"No, of course not," Leia replied, going back into proper princess mode. "I was obsessed with saving you. Your dick just happened to be the tool to accomplish that."

Han gave Leia one of his classic scoundrel smirks. "Well, Your Worship, this tool is ready to be used again." His cock expanded inside Leia, ready for round two.

Leia gasped. She never expected him to have such a quick recovery time. They were going to have so much sex. Yes! Oh no, she was being super-horny again. Oh, who cared? She was reunited with Han. She could be as horny as she wanted.

"Huh huh huh." A familiar chuckle echoed throughout the chamber.

"I know that laugh," Han said.

Jabba's slab slid forward, bringing him into view. Leia couldn't believe he was awake. She had given him enough sleeping powder to fell a bantha. Though maybe Jabba's fat reserves were so massive he was able to fight off the effects.

Gawhorrean Guards grabbed Han and Leia and hauled them to their feet. Han's cock slipped out of Leia, bringing with it more of her princess juices. She wanted to cover up her stained thighs, but the guards pinned her arms to her sides.

Han was in a similar state, cum dripping from his impressive space cock. What an embarrassing way for them to be captured.

"Look, Jabba," Han began, launching into his trademark con artist voice.

But Jabba was having none of it. He ordered the guards to take the smuggler-turned-rebel away.

Leia reached out to her love, but the pig men yanked her back. She gazed longingly at Han, their reunion much too fleeting.

The Gawhorreans marched her up to their gross boss, who

stared lustily at Leia.

She gulped. She had a feeling she was in a whole heap of trouble.

Chapter 2

Leia hung in the air, her arms suspended above her by chains. She was naked and dangling above a huge phallic instrument.

Boobla and Lay Me were on either side of her, in similar predicaments. Jabba had decided all three girls would be punished for freeing his favorite palace decoration. And that punishment would be impaling them on sex toys in front of Jabba's cronies.

Leia's chains were attached to a pulley system. A Gawhorrean held the other end of the chain and could raise and lower Leia at his master's command.

And his master decided it was a good time to issue such a command. Jabba barked at the guard, who released the chain.

Leia dropped, just enough so the phallic toy could penetrate her opening. "Ohhhh!" she cried. "Fuck, it's so big!" The fake cock was attached to a pole that extended several feet off the ground. And Leia was suspended above it, which gave all the palace residents a great view of her naked writhing.

Which she did when the guard lowered her a little more. "Uhhhhh, couldn't we start out with a smaller toy?" she pleaded.

Jabba grumbled in reply and Peepio translated. "Mistress Leia, the horny Jabba says he knows you secretly love huge cocks."

Leia gasped. How did Jabba know that? She was just discovering it herself. In reality, she was happy with pretty much any cock, though meaty ones like Han's were really nice. She couldn't wait to feel Han's manhood inside her again, his warm body pressing down on her.

But for now she had to take the penis-shaped toy that was slowly impaling her. And not-so-slowly driving her wild. It was huge, but it also touched all her sensitive princess parts just right. Which made it hard to contain her moans.

Jabba's minions didn't want her to contain them. They cheered every desperate cry and sex face she made. That was both embarrassing and enticing. Part of Leia liked being exhibited for these scoundrels and wanted them to ogle her bound, nude flesh.

She shook her head, trying to restore the proper princess part of her. Horny Leia had become very dominant over the more reserved version she usually portrayed to people. But when she was getting fucked constantly, how was she not supposed to be horny. Especially with two beautiful Twe'erk girls getting fucked alongside her.

Boobla and Lay Me were sliding down their respective artificial cocks, whimpering and moaning and looking sexier than any women in the galaxy, which was the special talent of all Twe'erk girls.

Jabba growled more orders, and the pig-faced guards lowered all three captives until they were fully impaled.

Leia let out a voiceless gasp. Every inch of her vagina was filled by the delicious dildo. It dominated her so much, she couldn't think about anything except how she needed to be fucked by it until she came all over herself.

Luckily, that's exactly what Jabba ordered his guards to do. They yanked the chains up and down, making Leia and the Twe'erk girls fuck themselves on the fake cocks.

Since she was chained and suspended in mid-air, Leia was completely helpless. She had to fuck the dildo at the speed and strength Jabba commanded. She had been reduced to a fuck toy for the Butt's amusement.

She would have been furious except that it felt amazing. Every time the guard lowered her onto the shaft, she thought she might black out from pleasure overload.

Her breasts were bouncing, her juices were squirting, and she was crying out in ecstasy. Dammit, why did she have to enjoy being a slut so much? And an exhibitionist slut at that. The crowd below her were absolutely loving her desperate gyrations. And those of the Twe'erk women as well.

Boobla and Lay Me had distinct but equally sensual moans, and both were skilled at spilling their salty spray down their legs, much to the delight of the onlookers.

Leia was delighted by it too: she was extremely turned on by her new friends and hoped Han would be up for some four-way fun with the girls. How could he not? He was a pirate with a vigorous libido. It'd probably be a dream come true. Though Leia wanted to have some alone time with him first. They needed to make sweet love, sharing sweet smooches and gentle caresses. After plenty of that, then Lay Me and Boobla could teach them how to get kinky.

Of course, Leia was getting plenty of lessons in that, thanks to all the debauchery Jabba was putting her through. She never knew she could have such powerful climaxes until she came to his palace and got fucked by so many creatures.

The creature fucking her now, or at least controlling how she was fucked, was quite excited by her squirming. The pig guard yanked the chain harder and faster, making Leia flop around on the cock like a rag doll.

"I... f... feel like a total fuck toy!" Leia told her colorful friends.

"Isn't it great?" Lay Me replied.

"My pussy's so stuffed!" Boobla cried.

Leia marveled at the Twe'erk girls. They seemed to have no problem being tied up and fucked. Leia had to admit it was pretty fun. Maybe she should forget about how embarrassed she was and just enjoy getting her pussy pounded.

Her pussy agreed as it chose that moment to have a galactic-sized orgasm.

"Ohhhhhhhhhh!" she squealed, her juices soaking the dildo and running down her legs. They formed a puddle on the floor, seeping into the two succulent pools formed by Boobla and Lay Me. The trio created an impressive lake of slutty sauce.

The Gawhorrean let the chain go slack, so Leia was fully impaled on the cock. She panted and squirmed, futilely kicking her legs out to try to find something to place her feet on. But she was six feet off the ground and had no choice but to sit on the big cock.

The other guards lifted Boobla and Lay Me off their sex toys and unchained them. The girls held on to each other to keep their legs from giving out.

Leia remained bound and stuffed. "Hey, what about me?" she asked Jabba.

"Chuba nabba raffa mabba," Jabba replied. "Chuba ra slutta."

"The most infallible Jabba says you are to remain chained," Peepio tittered.

Jabba roared and whacked the droid.

"Ohhh!" Peepio cried. "I am sorry your royal hugeness. Jabba also reminds the princess that she is a huge slut."

Leia's cheeks turned red. He didn't have to announce that to everyone. And it was even more embarrassing with Peepio saying it. The protocol droid's proper way of speaking made the slut accusation feel even dirtier. Not that it was erroneous:

she had been pretty slutty since she had arrived in the palace. If they just stopped shoving sexy cocks, fingers, and tongues inside her, she'd stop being so slutty.

"So I have to stay impaled on this huge sex toy?" Leia asked.

"Huh huh huh," Jabba chortled, then relayed instruction to the golden droid.

"Yes," Peepio told her. "But do not worry, Mistress Leia. Jabba says he will keep you occupied."

"Oh, good," Leia said in relief. "Wait, what does that me... holy space vibrators!!!" The phallic instrument rumbled to life within her, shaking her pussy so hard, it had no choice but to release more of its succulent juices.

Leia flailed on the vibrating device, her boobs bouncing, her ass shaking, and her pussy leaking. How did Jabba procure such decadent devices? Oh right, he was a crime lord. He could likely obtain any illicit item he wanted. He certainly had good taste in sex toys: this one was hitting Leia in all her ultra-horny spots.

Jabba instructed the band to strike up the music, and his minions went about their usual business, treating Leia like a lovely palace decoration to enjoy in the background.

Leia moaned as she was fucked out of her mind. First, Jabba had used a frozen Han to decorate his walls. Now, she was a bound fuck toy meant to entertain his retinue. She was really going to give it to this big Butt. And by that, she meant give him her pussy to lick a whole bunch. Wait, what? Oh no, she was succumbing to his sneaky plan to become his willing sex slave. She had to get out of here before she became so lost in lust all she could think about was getting fucked. But first, she would enjoy the endless orgasms she was having. They were really nice and gave her spicy tingles all over.

Jabba left her up there while he conducted business with the different criminal factions on Titooine who came to visit. He activated the vibrator during their negotiations to get favorable deals: it was well known all criminals loved seeing a helpless princess cum all over herself.

Leia couldn't believe her orgasms were being used as a negotiating tool. Though the diplomat in her appreciated Jabba's shrewdness. Perhaps she should get naked and be fucked during all future dealings with planets who provided much needed supplies to the Rebellion. The ragtag organization was always running short on credits and had barely managed to stay one step ahead of the Empire. If acting slutty helped bring freedom to the galaxy, then that's what Leia would have to do.

Jabba finally freed her from her shackles and had his guards lower her from the vibrator.

"Chuba wabba labuda, princess," he chortled.

"His Horniness says you are the most impressive squirter he's ever seen," Peepio translated.

"Oh, thank you," Leia replied, blushing. Then realized

what she was doing. "I mean, how dare you tie me up and treat me like a sex toy, making me have more amazing orgasms than I've ever had in my life." She put her hands on her hips, once again accidentally shaking her impressive bosom.

Jabba chuckled, likely amused by Leia's confession of how well the Butt lord could make her climax.

Leia crossed her arms and pouted, which smooshed her breasts together all sexy like. The huge space slug always had the upper hand on her. But Leia would have the last laugh. Good always triumphed over evil, even if it took a million orgasms by slutty princesses to make that happen.

Jabba licked his fat lips and spoke to his concubine.

"Mistress Leia," Peepio said. "The magnificent Jabba wants to know if you intend to stop causing mischief and be a good girl."

Leia turned up her nose. "Certainly not. I'll never yield to such a vile creature."

Jabba barked at one of his guards, who immediately spanked Leia's shapely bottom.

"Ack!" she yelped. The Gawhorreans had meaty hands that were perfect for giving firm spankings.

She turned on her attacker. "How dare you spank my royal b... oww!!" Another guard spanked her.

Before she could round on him, she was bent over a table and every pig man in the palace took turns dishing out powerful ass slaps.

"Ow, ow, ow, ow, owww!!" she cried. The spankings stung but also felt nice. She was discovering how much she enjoyed getting disciplined. "O... okay, I'll be a good girl!" she squealed after a particularly hard booty whack.

Peepio shuffled forward. "The benevolent Jabba is happy to hear that. But he enjoyed watching you get spanked so much that he has decided to make it a daily ritual, where all palace residents will get a turn disciplining your rear end."

"What?!" Leia gasped. "Oh c'mon, I said I'd be good."

"Jabba believes it is good to watch your luscious bottom get spanked."

Leia sighed. Why did she have to have such a hot butt? Usually, she was happy to get compliments on it, but she didn't realize its curviness would turn her into a spank toy.

So she got her ass slapped by every odd creature in the palace, which left her with one sore booty and one horny pussy. Spankings really turned her on.

After that, Boobla and Lay Me washed her and gave her another of their wonderful massages. It was almost worth going through all the naked embarrassment to get the Twe'erk girls to run their deft fingers over her skin.

Speaking of being naked, Leia and the girls were ordered to remain that way for the rest of the day as punishment for freeing Han.

So Leia was chained to Jabba fully nude, displaying her

princess goodies for all to see, something she was getting quite used to doing.

But she had learned how to manipulate her new master. If she rode his tail really hard, he would cum and pass out from exhaustion.

And that's exactly what she did, acting like a bantha rodeo girl and making Jabba climax multiple times.

When he was sound asleep, she managed to slip away and woke Boobla and Lay Me.

The blue girl fluttered her lovely violet eyes open. "Oh, hi. Do you want another three-way?"

Her green friend, who was wrapped in Lay Me's arms, popped her eyes open. "I'm up for a three-way."

"Um, thanks, girls," Leia replied. "That's sweet. But not right now. I need to see Han. Can you help me sneak in to where they're holding him?"

"Ooh, are you going to fuck him?" Lay Me asked.

"And can we watch?" Boobla echoed.

Leia tingled. These girls were obsessed with sex. "Well, the main goal is to get out of here. But I'm really horny from all the spankings, so we'll probably have sex and, yup, you can watch." Leia was certain Han would be fine with that. Who didn't like having aliens watch during sexy times?

Lay Me sat up and stretched, her magnificent boobs thrusting out at Leia. "Then we'll definitely help."

Boobla also stretched, competing with her friend for best

tit thrusting. "Though we would have helped either way. You're our favorite human."

Leia smiled. "Oh, thank you. You're my favorite Twe'erks."

"Yay!" The girls pulled Leia into a hug, where three pairs of naked breasts smashed together, which made Leia's nipples harden. Now she really had to fuck Han.

"Let's go," Leia whispered, carefully making her way through the sleeping palace residents.

It was time to fuck a scoundrel.

Chapter 3

It wasn't difficult to gain access to Han.

Boobla and Lay Me knew the location of the palace cells. And while they were guarded by Gawhorreans, Leia and the girls easily convinced the pig men to let them pass by giving them blowjobs.

Leia had learned a lot from her first time sucking a pig man's dick, and she had the guard grunting and snorting and spewing his thick spunk down her throat in no time.

She swallowed it like a good girl, which she had promised Jabba she'd be. But also because she knew the guard was more likely to let her pass if she acted like his sperm was yummy. It actually wasn't anywhere near as unpleasant as Leia had feared. It was musty and earthy but palatable. It got her wondering what Han would taste like. She was eager to find out.

The guards let them into the cell, locking it behind them.

"Han!" Leia flung herself onto her lover, embracing him tightly.

"Leia, you're naked!" he exclaimed.

"Oh, um, yeah, it's a long story. Has your vision

returned?"

"Not yet."

"I'll help you." She guided his hands down her back until they reached her buttocks. "Squeeze here."

He did, seizing her ass like it was the deed to his ship. She gasped and clutched his shirt, happy to be pressed against him and equally happy to let him feel her up.

"When did you get so frisky, Princess?" he asked.

"Since I arrived here. My eyes have really been opened wide." Her legs had been opened wide too, but she decided it wasn't the best time to tell him that. "Now get back to fondling me."

"Yes, Your Worship," he replied with a grin, happily squeezing Leia's delectable derriere.

A huge shape emerged from the shadows, letting out a warbling roar.

"Hi, Chewie," Leia said over Han's shoulder. Chewfucca was Han's co-pilot and most loyal friend. He was a Wookie, a tall, fur-covered race of tree dwellers, though Chewie spent most of his time in space. He was a fine pilot and an expert mechanic. He had also sworn a life-debt to Han and would do anything for the lovable scoundrel.

Leia had come to Titooine with Chewie, her furry friend pretending to be captured by Leia's bounty hunter persona, so they could gain access to Jabba's palace. Chewie had been thrown in a cell while Leia tried to rescue Han. Of course, that hadn't gone exactly to plan, and Leia had spent most of her time being a sex toy. She hoped Chewie hadn't been too lonely down here. "Are you okay?" she asked the Wookie.

He warbled again, ruffling Han's hair. Leia didn't speak Wookie, but she got the gist: Chewie was happy to be reunited with Han. So was she.

Chewie also didn't seem fazed to see Leia naked. Probably because his species never wore clothes. Their fur covered everything and kept them nice and toasty.

The friendly walking carpet tilted his head toward the Twe'erk girls.

"Oh, these are my friends, Boobla and Lay Me," Leia said. "They're Jabba's dancing girls. They helped me free Han from the carbonite."

Han gave Leia's ass a sinful squeeze. "Speaking of that, were you having sex with me when I unthawed?"

Leia's face flushed. "Um, yes. The panel was broken, so it was the only way to free you."

"The princess was very vigorous in her lovemaking to you, Mr. Space Pirate," Boobla told Han.

"She loves your cock," Lay Me added.

A huge grin spread across Han's face. "Really?"

Leia rolled her eyes. Oh boy, they had just given him a big head. Well, an even bigger one than he already had. He'd probably expect to fuck Leia anytime he wanted now. Actually, Leia had no problem with that. She'd gladly spread her legs for him whenever he requested. She wanted his strong arms around her and his strong cock inside her.

She patted Han's chest. "Yes, really. In fact, do you think we could..." Her fingers crept down his chest and underneath his waistband until they settled on his manhood. She took it gently in her hand and slowly stroked it. She would have never been this forward with him before. She had actually played hard to get in the past, pretending she didn't have feelings for him. But now they were in love, so there was no point in hiding her desires. She wanted Han. Wanted to lay with him and share their most intimate fluids.

He grabbed her buttocks firmly. "Sure thing, Your Worshipfulness."

Chewie let out a growl.

"Oh, sorry, pal," Han replied. "I forgot we were all stuck in the same cell."

"Girls?" Leia inquired of the Twe'erks.

"Don't worry," Lay Me said. "We'd be happy to take care of your furry friend."

"Yes!" Boobla agreed. "I can't wait to search through all that hair to find his big cock."

Leia's eyes widened. She had never thought about Chewie's cock. It was hidden beneath all his fur, but she didn't doubt it was big based on his huge size. But if any women were up for the challenge of a big, furry dick, it was Boobla and Lay Me.

"Have fun, pal," Han told his longtime friend.

The girls led Chewie to a darkened corner of the cell and giggled as their hands roamed his fur.

Leia took her lover's hands and brought him to the opposite corner, where she wrapped her arms around his neck and kissed him.

"I've missed you so much," she told him after their lips parted.

"Thanks for coming to rescue me," he replied.

"I'll always rescue you."

"Hey, that's my line."

She smiled and smooched him again. Han shivered against her. At first, she thought it was from her passionate kisses, but then she realized it was from the hibernation sickness.

"Take your clothes off and press your body against me," she instructed. "I'll warm you up."

Han didn't have to be asked twice. He hurried out of his garments with Leia's help, and they embraced tightly, plastering their nude forms to each other.

Leia rested her head against his chest and sighed. This was what she'd always wanted, to be held tenderly by Han and feel his heart beating against hers.

She also felt something else: Little Han sprouted straight up, rubbing against her stomach.

She gazed up at him with a smile. "Someone's happy to see me."

"I wish I could actually see you," he responded. "I've never seen a naked princess before."

"You never snuck any peeks at nubile royals on all the planets you've visited."

"Normally I was trying to get off planet as fast as possible before the authorities caught up to me."

Leia nodded. That made sense. And she was glad she was the first princess he had been with. That made her feel special.

He pressed his fingers into her lower back. "Besides, none of those princesses could come close to approaching your beauty."

She gasped, letting her body melt into him. She never knew he could be so romantic. She loved scruffy nerf herders!

"Oh Han, take me!" She leapt up, wrapping her legs around his hips and sank onto his impressive shaft.

"Ohhhhhhh!" they moaned in unison.

Leia lowered herself to the base of Han's penis, trembling against him. She loved his carbonite cock. But it was a million times better now: his penis was warm and agile and throbbed wonderfully within her.

"Leia, you're so tight!" he cried.

She squeezed his dick and kissed him. That's exactly what she wanted to hear. "Fuck my tight pussy with your huge cock!"

Han pressed her against the wall and thrust in and out of her.

Leia clung to him with her arms and thighs, blissfully enjoying every smooth penetration into her princess pussy.

She closed her eyes and gave herself over to him. This was their first time making love for real, and she wanted to savor every second of it.

She blinked her eyes open for a moment and glanced over Han's shoulder. On the other side of the room, Boobla and Lay Me were on their knees, both attacking Chewie's cock. The Wookie had a large paw on either woman's head, guiding them in their noble task of draining his furry balls.

Leia closed her eyes again and smiled. She was glad Chewie was having his own fun while she and Han made love. And the Twe'erk girls too. She knew they were happy to have sex with any species they came across.

Han went harder, his space cock penetrating deep inside her. She moaned in his ear, wanting him to know how much pleasure he was providing.

The wonderful feeling of climax soon welled within her, and her pussy began its pre-orgasmic spasms.

"I... I'm going to cum!" she wailed.

"I know!" Han replied.

He released his seed into her at the same moment she let her own juices flow. Their tanginess mixed together, one stream going in, the other going out.

Leia trembled as Han pumped more and more of his sperm into her. She loved the warm feeling of him filling her:

her pussy knew it was the proper home for his seed.

He finally pulled out, and she slid off his hips. His cum dripped from her cunt, running down her thighs.

He held her tightly, their bodies intertwined.

Leia shivered against him, the effects of her orgasms still flowing through her.

"I love you," she told him.

She put a finger to his lips before he could reply. "And don't say 'I know.'"

He smiled. "I love you, Leia."

They kissed for a long time, their naked bodies perfectly melding.

Leia was breathless after their smooch session. Han really knew how to kiss. There was no doubt in her mind that she wanted to be with him forever.

Across the room, Boobla and Lay Me climbed off a prone Chewie. Both girls were covered head-tail to toe in Wookie seed.

"Chewie can really cum!" Lay Me said happily, licking a drop off her leeku.

"He drenched us!" Boobla said just as excitedly.

"Have fun, pal?" Han asked his friend.

Chewie clambered to his feet and roared in satisfaction. Leia wasn't surprised. How could you not have fun with two gorgeous Twe'erk girls fucking you?

Boobla pointed at Leia's thighs. "Ooh, you coated the

princess really good."

"You should tie her up next time," Lay Me advised. "She gets super-slutty when she's bound."

Han's eyes perked up. "Really?"

Leia blushed furiously. "Stop sharing my slutty secrets!" she chided her naked friends. "Um, I mean, I'm not slutty and have definitely not been doing anything naughty."

Han smirked. "I knew there was a bad girl underneath all that prudishness."

"I am not prudish!" Leia pouted.

"You definitely proved that with all your desperate moans," Han replied.

Leia wrinkled her nose. "I hate you."

He pulled her in more tightly. "You love me."

"Okay, fine, I love you. Now kiss me."

Han happily complied, and Leia enjoyed his lips and the way his hands roamed her body. She had a feeling Han would have no problem finding out she had learned how to be slutty the past several days. In fact, he probably couldn't wait to tie her up and have his way with her. Leia couldn't wait either. She wanted to be helpless and give her body fully to the love of her life.

The guards barked at them, indicating the girls' conjugal visits were over.

Leia took Han's hands in hers. "I have to go, but don't worry, we'll get out of here soon."

"How?" he asked.

She squeezed his palms. "Our secret weapon is about to arrive.

She left him with a loving kiss, then scurried out.

Boobla and Lay Me rubbed their head-tails against Chewie and kissed his fur.

He patted their tushes, giving them an affectionate roar.

They followed Leia out, and the guards escorted them down the dank corridor.

"It's fun fucking a Wookie," Lay Me exclaimed.

"I hope we get to ride his furry dick again," Boobla agreed.

Leia smiled. She was certain they would once they escaped. Chewie was obviously taken with the two lovely Twe'erks. And they couldn't have asked for a nicer mate than Han's hairy friend.

Boobla snatched Leia's arm. "Did you have fun with your space pirate?"

Leia hopped up and down. "It was wonderful!"

Lay Me grabbed her other arm. "Did you enjoy his big dick?"

"It was amazing. He filled me with so much cum!" Leia gasped. Since when did she blurt out extremely naughty things like that? And in such an exuberant way? Was she becoming a nymphomaniac? Or was it her absolute love for Han? Probably a little of both.

The girls walked arm in arm, giggling about their manly

mates and the size of their courageous cocks.

The guards chained Leia back to Jabba, who was still sleeping and was none the wiser about Leia's nightly escapade.

She laid back against his slimy skin and tried to get some sleep. She needed to be well-rested for their break-out attempt tomorrow.

Jabba was about to get an unexpected guest.

Chapter 4

Leia was back in her slave girl outfit, lying on the dais beneath Jabba. That was his preferred place for her: he liked showing everyone she was his conquest.

She fidgeted and adjusted her breechcloth. Her secret weapon should have been here by now.

Then she sensed him. She couldn't quite explain it, but she always knew when he was near, like on Cloud City after he had lost his hand.

A black-cloaked figure entered the main palace chamber.

Two Gawhorrean Guards stepped forward to block his path.

The man raised his hand toward one, then the other.

Both guards collapsed into unconsciousness.

The intruder approached the dais and pushed back his hood.

Leia smiled. It was Luke Clitalker, one of her best friends and a fellow leading figure in the Rebel Alliance.

Luke had come a long ways since his farm boy days on Titooine. He now carried himself with a confidence he didn't possess when he had helped rescue Leia from the Empire's clutches four years ago.

He was dressed fully in black and had short brown hair above a boyish face that belied his power. Luke was a Jedi Knight and possessed the power of the Force, a sort of mystical energy that Leia didn't fully understand. She had heard stories of the Jedi from her parents, but they had supposedly died out long ago. Many believed they were nothing but myth.

Luke proved otherwise. Leia had seen him use his powers on countless occasions, always for noble purposes. Luke was honest and kind. Leia might have been attracted to him except she viewed him like a little brother, even though they were the same age. In fact, even when she kissed him that one time to make Han jealous, it felt weird, like she was making out with a relative.

Which is why her smile turned to a blush when Luke looked at her. She was embarrassed he was seeing her in such a scandalous outfit. But at least she wasn't naked. That would have been mortifying.

Luke quickly averted his gaze, focusing on Jabba, who had just woken up with a belch.

He verbally sparred with the big Butt, demanding the release of Han, Leia, Chewie, and their droids.

During the war of words, Leia learned that Jabba wasn't susceptible to Jedi mind tricks, which Leia was sure Luke had used to make his way into the palace. He had told her that a

Jedi can influence the will of the weak-minded.

That apparently wasn't Jabba. The gangster refused Luke's entreaties and pulled a sneaky trick. He opened a trap door underneath Luke, sending the Jedi tumbling into the pit below.

A grate closed over the opening to the pit, and the dais slid forward, giving Jabba a better view.

Leia gazed through the grate worriedly, trying to locate Luke in the dimly lit dungeon.

He clambered to his feet and dusted himself off, looking none the worse for wear.

Leia sighed in relief, but that was soon replaced with apprehension as a large gate on the other side of the pit lifted, revealing a huge creature.

It was a rancor. Leia had read about them but had never seen one in person. It was even more ferocious than she could have imagined. The creature was over five meters tall, had a gaping maw with huge teeth, and possessed razor-sharp claws that could easily tear virtually any species apart. It was reptilian-looking but lumbered on two legs instead of four. And those two legs were taking it straight toward Luke.

Leia tried to get closer to the grate to get a better angle, but Jabba yanked her back.

He lifted her breechcloth with his tail and rubbed it along her slit.

"Oh... ohhhhh!" she gasped. "Th... this isn't the time for

fucking. My friend's in danger."

Jabba disagreed, massaging Leia's lips harder and making her wet.

Leia clutched his tail, helping Jabba guide it along her lips. She could never resist his tail fuckings. He was too skilled at making her desperate to have an orgasm.

He pushed Leia forward with his tail, so she was on her hands and knees, bent over with her face by the grate.

He alternated between spanking her and rubbing her clit. Which made Leia feel very submissive, but at least she had an excellent view of what was happening down in the pit.

Luke nimbly dodged the rancor's swipes, which just enraged the creature even more.

Leia was worried for her friend but was a little distracted by Jabba's pussy persistence. He used his tail to spank her clit, which made it impossible for her to hold in her climax.

"Ohhhhhhhhh!" she screamed, spraying her juices across the grate.

Luke looked up, distracted by her cries.

"Ohhh, look out for the rancor!" she yelled, trying to disguise her sexual shrieks. Fortunately, only her upper body was visible through the grate, so Luke didn't know what Jabba was doing to her down below. She'd be so embarrassed if a Jedi Knight knew she loved getting fucked by a space slug.

Luke picked up a giant bone, likely the remains of a former meal of the rancor, and swung it at the beast.

That didn't deter the creature, who tried to chomp its small quarry. Luke shoved the bone in its massive maw, propping its jaws open.

The rancor backed off momentarily but then closed its mouth, shattering the bone and dripping saliva everywhere.

As Luke tried to elude its grasp, Jabba continued to play with Leia's pussy, keeping a constant stream flowing from between her legs. She muffled her screams so as not to distract her friend again.

Lusto emerged beside her, putting a comforting hand on her shoulder. He smiled at her, like he was letting her know he was there to help.

But then she noticed where his other hand was: down his pants. He was jerking off while watching Jabba fuck her. Freakin' Lusto! She was going to kick him in his space balls when they got out of here.

Jabba barked at Lusto, and the handsome former smuggler lifted Leia's breechcloth and draped it across her back, giving him and Jabba a clear view of her bare ass.

"What do you think you're doing?" Leia accused him.

"Sorry, Princess, Jabba's orders. He wants to see your ass shake while he makes you cum."

Right at that moment, Jabba flicked her clit and made her squirt even more powerfully.

"Fuck, I love cumming!" she confessed. The rancor roared at the same moment, covering up her screams. Leia was glad of that. She was coming dangerously close to Luke finding out she had become a big slut. She only wanted Han to know that. She also wanted Han to treat her like a big slut and fill her with his space seed a bunch more.

Jabba chortled behind Leia.

"The melodious Jabba says princesses are quite skilled at shaking their asses," Peepio translated.

Leia could only moan in response. She couldn't stop her royal butt from shaking with how much she was cumming. Jabba had really done a number on her clit.

So he and Lusto got a nice booty-shaking show, much to the delight of both males based on their lewd grunts.

Leia was so busy squirting she nearly missed Luke's amazing display of dexterity.

He hurled a rock at the door sensor and hit it straight on.

The huge metal gate came crashing down on the rancor, who was passing just beneath it, crushing the fearsome creature.

Leia let out a sigh of relief. Then let out some sexy juices.

Jabba wasn't so happy. He roared in anger at the defeat of his pet monster.

Several guards entered the dungeon and took Luke into custody.

Jabba yanked Leia back to him, ceasing his tail fucking.

Leia knew he must be irate if he didn't want to play with her pussy. He had been obsessed with it ever since he had captured her.

Jabba barked more orders, and his retinue began making preparations for a sojourn beyond the palace walls.

Leia bit her lip. It looked like they were going on a field trip. But likely not on one that involved a nice picnic.

She had a bad feeling about this.

Chapter 5

Leia stood next to Jabba, peering out the thin-slitted windows of the large sail barge.

They were skimming over the sand dunes of Titooine, approaching the domain of the fucklacc, a creature that made the rancor look tame.

The fucklacc was supposedly over a hundred meters long, though it liked to burrow underground, so only its mouth was visible, which it used to gulp down anyone unfortunate enough to come across it.

On their journey across the dunes, Jabba had told Leia that the fucklacc had a special power: it would provide non-stop orgasms to its prey for a thousand years.

Leia's pussy had spasmed upon hearing that. She couldn't process cumming for that long. And how was it even possible? Did the fucklacc have special nutrients that kept people alive while it fed off their cum. And while it might not sound like a terrible fate, a thousand year orgasm would be too much for anyone, even a super-slut like her. Wait, what? Dammit, she had to stop calling herself that. Unless Han liked it, then she'd call herself any dirty name he wanted. But first she had to save him and the others from a terrible orgasmic fate. If anyone was going to make Han cum non-stop, it was going to be her, not some gross monster.

On the way to the fucklacc pit, Jabba had demanded his concubine pleasure him. So Leia grinded on his tail until he came. And then climbed atop his face and let him lick her cunt until she squirted into his huge mouth.

While he was giving her oral, he made her confess that she was a dirty whore and several other embarrassing things. Leia couldn't stop herself when she was in the throes of orgasmic delight. Jabba knew how to push her buttons, especially the pronounced button that escaped her hood whenever he licked her.

By the time they reached the fucklacc pit, Leia was sweaty and covered in her own juices. Being a sex slave was hard work.

Jabba let Boobla and Lay Me clean the princess from a nearby bucket of water while keeping a tight grip on the chain attached to her collar.

"You're getting so good at being slutty," Boobla told Leia.

"You're a natural whore," Lay Me agreed.

Leia smiled. "Oh, thanks. Hey, wait a minute, that's not a good thing. Is it?"

The green girl sponged Leia's right thigh. "It's a great thing."

Her blue friend sponged the left. "We love natural

whores."

Leia shrugged. "Oh, okay." She closed her eyes and let the Twe'erk women gently clean her. She supposed it could be considered a talent to immediately learn the ways of the slut. Her parents had always praised her for being a quick study. Though they probably never thought that would apply to her acting like a whore.

Tears spilled down her cheeks as memories came flooding back.

"What's wrong?" Boobla asked with concern.

"Are we going too hard?" Lay Me queried.

Leia wiped away the wetness. "N... no, it feels nice. I just... miss my family. The Empire took them from me."

The Twe'erk girls hugged her from either side, squishing her with their impressive bosoms.

"We'll be your family," Boobla said.

"We can all be sisters," Lay Me echoed. "Oh, um, maybe step-sisters because we still want to fuck you!"

Leia sniffled and embraced her new friends, kissing each on the cheek. "You girls are wonderful. I'm so happy I met you."

"And we're happy we met a horny princess," Lay Me replied.

Boobla nodded energetically.

Leia laughed and peppered their leeku with kisses, much to the delight of both women. There was nothing Twe'erks liked better than a sexy princess touching their head-tails.

They arrived at the Pit of Fuckoon, and Leia got her first glimpse of the fucklacc. Its mouth sat wide open within the dune pit. Its opening was so large it could easily have swallowed the sail barge. It had more serrated teeth than Leia could count, and several tendrils whipped around its mouth. Leia wondered if the creature liked to tie its prey up while giving them unending orgasms.

Several smaller skiffs zipped past the barge, filled with Jabba's minions. One of them held Han, Luke, and Chewie, imprisoned in shackles. Lusto was on their skiff as well, still masquerading as one of Jabba's guards. Hopefully, he'd do something useful besides jerk off to mental images of Leia's naked body.

Jabba had Peepio relay the prisoners' imminent demise at the hands, or tentacles, of the fucklacc.

The skiff's guards prodded Luke along a plank extending from the side of the small craft. He gazed down at the gaping maw of the monster but showed no fear. That's because he knew something Jabba didn't. And Leia knew it too.

They had a secret weapon on the sail barge: R6D9, the plucky astromech droid who was Peepio's longtime companion and who had been instrumental to the Rebellion's success. R6 had a cylindrical body, a rotating domed head, and three legs, which he used to zip around on his wheels. He also had lots of gadgets that emerged from his body whenever he needed them. Many of those gadgets were phallic-shaped. More than one female Rebel had confessed to Leia that she had asked R6 to pleasure her with his instruments, and that he was just as skilled at that as he was starship navigation. Leia had never used R6's gadgets that way, though she'd be lying if she said she had never been tempted. But the droid was like a best friend to Luke, so she didn't think it would be right. But she was glad R6 was providing sexual release to other ladies of the Rebellion. Ladies of the Rebellion? Now that was a great name for a holo-calendar. She could pose in her slave girl outfit and have Boobla and Lay Me wear their sexy dancers' clothing. Wait a minute, she was supposed to be helping run the Rebel Alliance, not thinking up how to sell sexy calendars. Of course, if those calendars helped fund the Rebels and let them take down the Empire, it'd be totally worth it. Plus, she kind of wanted an excuse to do a sexy photo shoot. Oh boy, she was becoming one saucy princess.

R6 had remained mostly in the background at Jabba's palace, fixing things and sometimes carrying drinks to the Butt lord's minions.

But now he was positioned at one of the barge's windows, waiting for the signal from Luke.

The Jedi Knight saluted and dropped off the plank toward the fucklacc's mouth. At the last moment, he grabbed the end of the plank and springboarded upward, performing a flying somersault and landing on the skiff.

At the same time, R6 launched Luke's lightsaber from within its body. It soared in a long arc toward the smaller craft.

Luke broke his restraints and extended his hand, using the Force to guide the lightsaber into his grasp. At least, Leia assumed he used the Force. Nothing else would explain how the lightsaber's trajectory changed so suddenly.

Luke ignited the brilliant green energy blade and attacked the guards on the skiff.

"Yes!" Leia cheered.

The rest of the sail barge's occupants weren't so happy. A confused panic broke out, with Jabba roaring in anger.

He tongue-spanked Leia hard, apparently blaming her for the sneaky shenanigans.

That was the last straw for the scantily clad princess. Jabba might have given her wonderful orgasms, but he was a vile creature who imprisoned innocent Twe'erk girls, and likely plenty of others. She had to use the confusion to make her move.

She used the weighted end of her chain to smash a nearby control panel, extinguishing the artificial lighting on the barge.

Shrieks from various creatures rang out as the ship was pitched into semi-darkness, the thin shafts of sunlight streaming through the window slits the only thing providing illumination.

The chain attached to Leia's collar was long, and she was

able to leap behind Jabba and wrap it around his huge neck.

She yanked with all her might, choking the big Butt. In the darkness and confusion, no one knew what she was doing.

Jabba flailed his stubby arms and gagged. His tail flopped excitedly. And then shot semen all over Leia.

She sputtered, not expecting a cum facial while choking him. Apparently, Jabba was into really kinky stuff. She should have known.

She decided to change tactics. She picked up the heavy end of the chain and bonked him over the head with it.

He made a strange Butt noise and fell unconscious.

A lightsaber ignited on the deck above, letting Leia know Luke had made his way to the main barge. She just hoped Han and Chewie were all right. And, okay, even Lusto. The last she had seen him, he had fallen from the skiff and was trying to climb up the sand away from the fucklacc's tentacles. She was sure Han would save him. Of course, maybe Lusto wouldn't mind a thousand-year orgasm.

She jumped off Jabba's perch just in time for R6D9 to roll up to her. A phallic object emerged from one of his compartments.

Leia held out her chain, and R6 zapped it with electricity, breaking her bonds. But the jolt also hit her clit, sending a different kind of electricity coursing through her body.

"Ohhhh fuuucckkkk!" she wailed, squirting all over R6.

She trembled on the floor, the electric shock sending a

bunch of mini-orgasms through her after the initial major climax. No wonder all the Rebel women wanted the droid to fuck them.

R6 let out a series of beeps, which was how he communicated. Luke could understand him, but Leia could only pick up a general tone or mood. This one sounded questioning.

She used her crimson breechcloth to wipe her cum off his shiny dome. "Sorry, R6. I didn't mean to cum all over you. But, um, think of it as a nice polishing."

The droid beeped happily, accepting that explanation.

Leia smiled. He was probably used to girls squirting on him. And she hadn't lied: he was shinier now that she had polished him with her cum. "Don't tell Luke I squirted all over you, okay?"

He replied with an affirmative beep. Apparently, R6 was good at keeping slutty secrets. He was an excellent little droid.

She made her way to the top deck, where Luke was fending off multiple attackers with his lightsaber.

Below them and off the starboard side, Han and Chewie were hauling Lusto onto the skiff. The horny scoundrel had evaded the fucklacc's mouth, though the same couldn't be said for several of Jabba's men. Leia assumed they had tumbled from the skiff into the Pit of Fuckoon since Han, Chewie, and Lusto had sole possession of the craft.

She was glad they were safe. And was equally glad her

Twe'erk friends were okay.

Boobla and Lay Me rushed up to her, their clothing singed but otherwise none the worse for wear.

"Girls, stay close to me," Leia ordered. "We're getting out of here."

The Twe'erks nodded, huddling together. They were great teachers when it came to sex, but when it came to taking command of a tense situation, they were happy to follow Leia's orders.

Leia leapt onto the large double-barreled gun that was mounted at the bow of the barge.

She activated the controls and rotated the barrels so they were pointing at the deck.

She fired, blowing a huge hole in the barge.

The ship creaked and titled, losing altitude as explosions broke out from within its belly.

Luke dispatched the last of the guards and grabbed a rope that was tied to the sails. "Leia, c'mon!"

Leia snatched Boobla's and Lay Me's hands and pulled them over to Luke. "These are my friends," she explained. "They're coming with us."

Luke gave them a quick once over. "I'm not sure I can carry all of you."

"Hey, are you saying we're fat?" Lay Me asked with a cute pout.

"That's not very nice, Mr. Jedi," Boobla added.

"No, no," Luke quickly replied. "I didn't mean... you both have amazing... um, that is..."

Leia patted the girls' leeku. "He merely meant it will be hard to swing us all on the rope without one of us falling. He thinks you're both ravishing."

The Twe'erks beamed at Luke, much happier with that assessment.

Luke sighed and shot Leia a silent nod of thanks.

She suppressed a giggle. It wasn't the first time she had saved him after he had put his foot in his mouth.

She grabbed his arm. "Luke, use the Force."

"Oh, right." He nodded sheepishly. Even though he was now a formidable Jedi Knight, he was still that innocent farm boy Leia had met all those years ago. She was glad he hadn't changed that much. His innocence was one of his best qualities. Of course, if Boobla and Lay Me got a hold of him, he might not be innocent for much longer.

Leia and the girls clambered around him on the rope, pressing their mostly nude bodies against him. Leia thought she saw his little lightsaber spring to action, but she turned away before it got to full mast. She just didn't feel right looking at Luke that way. Luckily, she was more than happy looking at Han's big cock all day long.

With the three ladies awkwardly strewn all over him, Luke cast off from the sinking barge, soaring through the air toward the skiff. Leia felt an unseen power on her legs and rear end preventing her from sliding off the rope. The Force was indeed strong with this one. Maybe Luke could use his powers to give Boobla and Lay Me incredible orgasms. The girls deserved to fuck a nice guy after being imprisoned by jerky Jabba.

Speaking of the slimy slug, the sail barge careened toward the Pit of Fuckoon. Leia wondered if the fucklacc would be able to digest a creature as rotund as Jabba. But she had more pressing concerns, like getting out of this desert.

They swung onto the skiff, landing gently.

Leia fell into Han's arms, giving him the most epic kiss of his life. At least, that's what she was going for. From his breathless reaction after their lips parted, she was pretty sure she succeeded.

"Let's go," Luke told Lusto, who was at the controls. "And don't forget the droids."

"We're on our way!" Lusto replied, piloting the skiff across the sand to where Peepio and R6 had fallen out of the barge.

They hauled the droids on board and flew across the dunes, far away from nasty Butts and scary tentacle creatures.

Chapter 6

Leia emerged from the cramped shower with a white towel wrapped around her hair and another around her body. That one was barely long enough to conceal her private areas. But compared to the skimpy slave girl outfit she had been forced to wear for a week, she felt like she was wearing her snowsuit from Hoth.

She was on Han's ship, the Millennium Whorecon. It's claim to fame: it was the fastest hunk of junk in the galaxy. But Han loved the ship, and it had gotten them out of more than one tight spot, so Leia had become fond of it too.

She plopped on a couch in the lounge area, right between Boobla and Lay Me, and sighed. It was nice to have a proper shower and get the stink of Jabba's palace off her. And not worry about being ogled by all his weird minions. Sure, it had made her horny and wet, and the sex was great. But she didn't want to spend the rest of her life as Jabba's sex slave. She wanted to be Han's sex slave. Well, at least pretend to be when they did sexy role-play.

Boobla and Lay Me also wore towels, the soft cloth wrapped cutely around their curvy bodies and curvy leeku.

Leia had let them shower first. They had been prisoners for much longer, so it was only right they get to cleanse themselves before her.

The blue and green ladies looked especially fetching with tiny droplets running down their bodies.

Boobla took Leia's left arm and Lay Me her right, both girls snuggling up against her.

"Thanks for rescuing us from Jabba!" Boobla said.

"You're our slutty hero!" Lay Me echoed.

"Oh, okay," Leia replied. "But do I have to be a slutty hero? Can't I just be a regular hero?"

Boobla shook her head. "Nope. You're way too slutty to be just regular."

"You're the sluttiest princess in the galaxy!" Lay Me agreed.

Leia wrinkled her nose. That wasn't really the title she was going for, but she knew the girls meant it as a compliment. And it's not like she hadn't earned it with how submissive she had been to Jabba and his minions. But was she really the sluttiest princess in the galaxy? There had to be other princesses on other planets who were huge whores. And she needed to meet those princesses and fuck them! Wait, what? Oh no, she really was a slutty princess. Hmm, well it would probably help her and Han's sex life. Space pirates definitely loved slutty princesses.

Lay Me traced her fingers up Leia's thigh. "Wanna fuck

again?"

Leia's eyes widened. "But we just showered."

"We can shower again after fucking," Boobla replied.

Leia considered that. It sounded logical, but she knew there was a limited supply of water on the Whorecon and they couldn't take an unlimited number of showers. There was also an even better reason to postpone another sex session with the Twe'erks. "I'd love to girls, but I want to spend some time alone with Han."

Lay Me nodded. "Oh, of course. I bet you're going to ride his bantha stick all night."

"I hope he fills you up with his creamy cum!" Boobla enthused, squeezing Leia's arm.

Leia blushed. "I... I hope so too." She wanted Han inside her so bad, wanted him to shoot all his manhood into her like she belonged to him.

As if on cue, Han strolled into the cabin. He had put on fresh clothes, similar to the ones he had been wearing but without a vest.

Leia smiled and rushed over to him, throwing her arms around his neck and peppering his lips with kisses. Ever since they had freed him, she couldn't stop kissing him. She wanted his body pressed against her all the time.

He moved his hands to the small of her back and pressed gently, eliciting a gentle gasp from her. She loved how strong his hands were and how he knew how to touch her just right.

Boobla yanked Lay Me off the couch. "Let's give them some alone time."

Her blue-skinned friend nodded. "Right. We can go to the cockpit and suck some cocks!"

They dropped their towels and sashayed out, shaking their colorful tushes. It looked like Lusto and Chewie were about to get a nice surprise.

Han watched the girls go, making it evident his sight had returned.

Leia turned his face back to her. "Hey, I want your focus on my rear end, not theirs."

He smirked. "I'd love to focus on your royal rear end, Your Hineyness."

She batted him playfully. "You think you're so funny."

"Right now, I think I'm so horny. This towel's barely covering you."

"Actually, I think it's covering too much." Leia took a step back and let the towel drop, revealing her breasts and pussy, both glistening with droplets of water.

She removed the towel from her head and shook her hair out, her damp brunette strands sticking to her back.

A large bulge formed in Han's trousers.

Leia smiled. She liked turning him on.

She walked slowly backward, beckoning him with her finger. Her breasts bounced softly with each step. Her hips swayed gently side to side. She had learned a lot from the

Twe'erk girls about how to entice a man.

Han got a big, goofy grin on his face, letting her know he was completely smitten.

She led him into the adjoining room, which housed the crew quarters. The sleeping arrangements consisted of three sets of double-decker bunks embedded in the walls. It wasn't great for privacy, but this was a cargo ship, not a luxury liner.

Fortunately, no one else was back there. Luke had flown off with R6 in his X-Wing, saying he had to visit an old friend but that he would meet them back at the fleet. And Peepio was in the cockpit, likely annoying Lusto and Chewie with his knowledge of boring trivia. Unless he was telling them all the slutty things Leia did in Jabba's palace. Lusto already knew a bunch of it, but he hadn't seen everything. And she didn't want him knowing any more than he already did. Peepio wouldn't spill the beans, would he? No, he was a proper protocol droid. He likely wanted to erase Leia's whorish behavior from his memory banks just as much as she did. Well, except for her sexy times with the Twe'erk girls. And fucking the two Gawhorrean guards. And Jabba's fantastic tongue. And... oh fine, she wanted to remember every single slutty detail.

But right now, she wanted to make new slutty memories with Han.

He pressed against her, her butt bumping against the console next to the nearest bunk. She kissed him and fumbled with his belt, desperately wanting to get his pants off.

He removed his shirt while she yanked his trousers and underwear down.

She gasped as his lively cock bounced up and down. It was even more impressive than when she saw it in Jabba's palace. Of course, the lighting was terrible there so she never got a proper look. But now she got to see it in its full glory. And it was yummy!

She wrapped her fingers around it and stroked. His body tensed and he grabbed her tightly.

"Oh Leia!" he moaned.

She kissed him some more and played with his cock. It was warm and girthy and felt just right in her fingers. She planned to give him a handjob every time she was in the co-pilot's seat. Or maybe a blowjob. Or maybe ride him like a bantha girl. There were so many ways she could fuck him in the cockpit.

Han eased her down onto the bunk. The mattress wasn't plush, but it was surprisingly comfortable. Her head hit the pillow, and Han climbed on top of her.

She closed her eyes and sighed as she felt the weight of his rugged body press down on her. And then he was inside her. Her whole body was filled with a warm, wonderful feeling. A feeling that this was the cock that would take ownership of her pussy.

She wrapped her arms around Han's neck and her legs

around his hips and moved in time with his thrusts.

Han pulled the bunk curtain closed and kissed her while they made love. It was everything she imagined it would be and a million light years better.

She let her body merge with Han's and lost track of the hours as they made non-stop love.

***

Eventually, she woke up. She had fallen asleep after being filled countless times by Han.

He was still asleep, sprawled on top of her. And his penis was still inside her. She didn't mind. It felt comfortable inside her cozy pussy.

She ran her fingers through his short hair and caressed his cheek. She wished she could stay like this forever and not have to fight the stupid Empire. But she would never shirk her duty and would never rest until the forces of evil were vanquished from the galaxy. She was just glad Han was by her side to help with the vanquishing.

She closed her eyes, content to listen to Han's rhythmic breathing, when the curtain was pulled aside.

"Oh, there you are, Mistress Leia," Peepio said. "I am glad I have located you."

"Peepio!" she yelped. "What are you doing? I'm naked!"

"Mistress Leia, might I remind you that I saw you naked

exactly sixty-two times in Jabba's palace. And you seemed quite pleased to be seen that way."

Leia's cheeks burned brightly. She didn't think anything would be more embarrassing than what she went through in Jabba's palace, but Peepio's frank assessment of the events there might have done the trick. She had no idea she had disrobed, or more accurately been stripped, that many times during her service to Jabba. Or that she had come across so eager to be ogled. But still, she couldn't have droids going around peeping on her whenever they wanted.

"Okay, that's technically accurate," she replied, unable to move as her sleeping lover's body was pinning her down. Han was apparently a sound sleeper. She was surprised after his long carbonite snooze that he could sleep so much. Guess she really tired him out with how much they fucked. Yes! Score one for the slutty princess. Okay, she really needed to stop calling herself that. "But now that I'm out of Jabba's clutches, I intend to wear clothes."

"I am relieved to hear it," the droid replied. "Though you don't seem to be following that intention right now."

Leia blushed some more. "That's because Han and I were... I mean, we had to... you see, we... oh, forget it, why did you need to find me?"

"I wanted to inform you that we will rendezvous with the fleet shortly."

"You needed to come down here and see me naked just to

tell me that?"

"Lusto thought you would like to hear the news from me. He insisted I deliver the message in person."

Leia rolled her eyes. Freakin' Lusto. He was probably laughing his ass off up in the cockpit, imagining Peepio interrupting Han and Leia's lovemaking. Maybe she could convince Chewie to toss him out the airlock. Or get Boobla and Lay Me to tie him up for kinky sex but then leave him with blue balls. That would show him.

"Okay, message delivered," Leia told the droid. "Can you, um, give us some privacy now?"

"Of course, Mistress Leia. Right after I inform Captain Solo." Peepio rapped his metal fingers on Han's back.

"Whu... wha?" Han asked groggily as he came to.

"Captain Solo, I have wonderful news! We are nearly at our destination."

Han took one look at the droid, then at a naked Leia, then back at Peepio. "Get the hell out of here, Goldenrod! We're trying to have sex!" He bonked Peepio on his metallic head and pulled the curtain shut.

"What an impossible man," Peepio complained as he shuttled off.

Han's frown turned to a smile as his eyes alighted on Leia. He brushed her hair behind her ear. "Hi, gorgeous."

She beamed at him. "Hi. Thanks for getting rid of the golden voyeur."

"No problem. Back at the fleet already, huh?"

Leia understood the disappointment in his voice. She wanted more alone time too.

She wrapped her arms around his neck. "Guess we better put the little time we have left to good use."

He smiled. "Guess so."

They kissed and made love all the way back to the Rebel fleet.

Leia knew they had a lot more work to do to defeat the Empire.

But, even more important, she had a lot more fucking to do.

May the Sex Force be with them!

Fully Nude and Erotic Covers are available on my Patreon page. You can get Nude and Sex Covers of this and other books as well as over two hundred naked/erotic pictures of my characters. Visit Patreon.com/RileyRoseErotica to check them out!

More Fun and Sexy Books

Star Sluts: Deep Space Sixty-Nine
Captain Cassidy Clitko and her crew of horny women travel to the final frontier, bringing peace by being the best sluts in the galaxy! With Commander Ju'sey Cocque, Doctor Bella "Boner" Boobstar, and Ensign Hannah "Hot Ass" Ho, it's never a dull moment on the USS Slutstream, the finest ship in Slutfleet. But when a Klingcock ship shows up and demands Cassidy honer their treaty with the United Federation of Sluts, the hot human captain must sexually satisfy every muscular futa woman on the alien ship. Check out Star Sluts: Where no slut has gone before!

Remy and the Sex Monsters
Remy Alvarez loves science-fiction. She just didn't expect to be living it! After leaving a movie marathon late at night, she's shocked to find herself on board an alien ship. And that all those myths about aliens loving to probe humans are true. And if banging aliens isn't enough, she discovers Bigfoot is real and loves having furry fun with naked co-eds. Plus, she gets a summer job with a cute and kooky scientist who wants Remy to test out a sex robot who thinks its mission is to turn college girls into submissive sluts. Will Remy be able to survive getting frisky with well-endowed aliens, tentacle girls, sexy scientists, hot MILFs, and sex-obsessed robots?

Submissive Princess: Royal Slut
Princess Aaylani is the most beautiful princess in the Seven Queendoms. To avert a war, she must marry Queen Jaiyanna of the neighboring nation of Sosha, a woman known for her kinky domination of her partners. With the help of her handmaiden Misty, Aaylani tries to prepare for the trials ahead by having Misty discipline her in extremely sensual ways and test out every sex toy in the palace on her tight princess parts. Will Aaylani be ready for the powerful queen? Find out how submissive this princess gets in this sexy erotic fantasy!

Sexy Time Cop: Cowgirl and Pirate Sluts
Riley Shu is a time cop, traveling to amazing periods in the past to stop criminals from altering the timeline. And having sex with some of the hottest men and women in history! The sexy time cop has to save Wyatt Earp and Doc Holliday from a future felon and gets in some kinky cowgirl fun along the way. Then it's off to the Caribbean and the Golden Age of Piracy for some submissive shenanigans with the most famous female pirate of all time: Anne Bonny! Will Riley's kinky fun change the timeline? Find out in Book 1 of this sexy, sci-fi journey through time!

Visit RileyRoseErotica.com to get a Free eBook and check out more of my sexy books!

E-mail: Riley@RileyRoseErotica.com

Facebook: RileyRoseErotica
Twitter: @RileyRoserotica
Instagram: @RileyRoseErotica

About the Author

Riley Rose writes comedic, sexy stories featuring fun-loving female protagonists who love taking their clothes off. Discover sexy sci-fi, fantasy, and action/adventure worlds in over forty books and Kindle Vella stories, featuring naughty witches, frisky fairy tale characters, sex-obsessed robots, and titillating tentacles. You'll find fun, friendship, and a ton of submissive sex in Riley's books. Join the sexy shenanigans! Find out more at RileyRoseErotica.com.

Printed in Great Britain
by Amazon